TEDDY
BEAR TALES

INDEX

This Book Belongs to

....

TEDDY'S DAY
AT THE SEASIDE

TEDDY'S DAY AT THE SEASIDE

It was early in the morning and the sun was shining brightly through the bedroom window. All the toys were in the corner and one little bear in particular was very excited. Teddy could not wait for everyone else to wake up.

"Hey!" he whispered excitedly to the other toys. "Guess what I'm going to do today. Lily is going to take me to the seaside! I heard her asking her mum if she could take me with her last night when she was going to bed and her mum said she could."

Lily was Teddy's little girl and this was the very first time that they would be going out of the house or even out of the garden!

Lily and her family packed up all their things for their day out and put them in the car ready for their journey. On the way to the seaside Lily sat in her seat and, because there was not a lot of room left, Teddy had to ride in the back of the car with the bags and the towels and all the other things for their day at the beach.

"This is a bit of a squeeze," thought Teddy. "I can't even stretch my paws."

Teddy was squashed between the bags and the beach ball and was wriggling about trying to get more comfortable but it was no use.

"And I can't even see much out of the window. I do hope we get there soon."

They soon arrived at the seaside and the warm breeze smelled of salt and seaweed. Up above, the seagulls were squawking and flying high in the sky. They all quickly unpacked and carried their things down on to the sand.

"Come with me," said Lily as she took Teddy's paw and they went to play.

"Here, catch!" she said, throwing a big, brightly coloured ball but Teddy was not very good at catching things and the ball rolled along the beach.

"Never mind," she said, "I think maybe we should do something else."

Then she made a big boat-shape in the sand for them to sail in the bright sunshine.

"I like Lily's boat," thought Teddy, "but it hasn't gone very far."

"Let's make some sandcastles," said Lily.

So they made lots of them and their best one was almost as big as Lily! It was a very fine sandcastle indeed and, right at the top, they put four bright flags which she had brought from home.

"I am the king of this castle," thought Teddy, standing proudly on top of the big sandcastle.

The little bear was so busy being king of the castle that he did not notice Lily going up the beach to get some ice-cream.

"I wonder where she has gone," said the little bear wistfully. "I hope she comes back for me soon."

Teddy waited for what seemed like a very long time and now noticed that the sea was getting closer. The tide was coming in!

Teddy jumped up and down and waved and shouted at Lily but she was too busy eating her ice-cream and all the time the waves were getting closer.

The waves were so close now that they were washing away the sand and the shells of Teddy's castle.

"Oh! What shall I do?" thought Teddy sadly. "She seems to have forgotten all about me. I will have to try and send her a signal."

Just then Teddy saw a jolly seagull flying overhead and had an idea.

"Ahoy there!" Teddy shouted to the seagull. "Can you help me? My little girl is over there on the beach and if she does not help me soon I shall be washed away."

"Of course I'll help you!" squawked the seagull. "What do you want me to do?"

"Here," said Teddy, holding out one of Lily's flags. "Give her this!"

The seagull swooped down and took the flag. He flew up the beach and dropped it over Lily. It fluttered down and landed in her ice-cream.

"Oh!" she cried. "How did that get here?"

She looked round but the seagull had flown away. As she looked she saw Teddy standing bravely on the castle with the sea all around it. Any minute now the sandcastle would be washed away.

She ran down the beach just in time to grab poor Teddy from the sandcastle as it melted into the sea and the other little flags floated away.

"Everything is all right now, Teddy dear," whispered Lily into Teddy's ear as she gave her little bear a hug. She held Teddy very close to her, tucked under her arm, as they went up the beach.

It was almost time to go home but first Lily rubbed Teddy's paws with a big towel until they were all dry and fluffy once again.

Then Lily said, "When we come to the seaside again it would be really nice to go in the water properly so I suppose I'll just have to teach you how to swim."

"I think I had better start off in the paddling pool at home," thought Teddy as she gave him a little squeeze. They packed up all their things and got into the car and, this time, Teddy sat on Lily's knee all the way home.

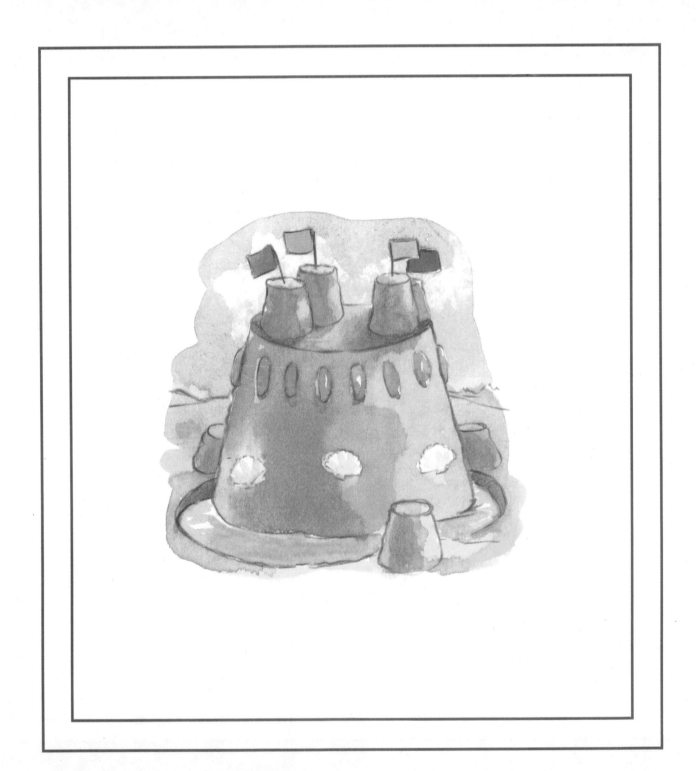

THE WISH

THE WISH

Late one night, high up in the attic, a lonely, little teddy bear sat and looked out of the window at the night sky. The teddy bear had been sitting in the attic for a long time. It had been a very long time since this bear had played with anyone. The children had all grown up long ago and did not have time for a teddy bear any more. Tonight there was a bright star twinkling in the sky and as he watched it the little bear made a wish. He closed his eyes and crossed his paws and said,

"Starlight! Star bright! Grant me a wish tonight. Let me have someone to play with please."

"I don't suppose it will work," Little Ted thought as he sat gazing at the star, "but you never know."

The next morning the little bear heard lots of noises. There was much banging about and footsteps on the stairs coming up to the attic.

"Oh dear! What's happening?" wondered Little Ted as someone came into the room. All the old toys and games were being packed into boxes. Little Ted was put in a big box with jigsaws and some old alphabet bricks.

"It's very dark in this box," he thought as the big box was taken downstairs. "I wonder where I'm going." There was lots of jiggling up and down and thumping and scraping. At last the box stopped moving and everything was quiet. Little Ted peeked out of the top of the box. He was not in the house any more! The box was on a table in the biggest room he had ever seen!

Soon lots of people came into the room. They were chatting and laughing as they unpacked the bags and boxes. As they sorted things out they were put on one of the tables. Each table had different things on it. One had lots of clothes, another had books and CDs and tapes.

Little Ted was put with other toys and games on a table next to the stall selling tea, coffee, scones and cakes.

Little Ted nudged the little elephant who was sitting next to him and whispered, "Do you know where we are?"

"We are in a hall and this is a jumble sale. I heard the man on the cake stall say so," the elephant replied. "I think they are going to sell us!"

The jumble sale opened at two o'clock with lots of people rushing in to see what bargains they could find. Little Ted could not count them all.

"I'd like a nice new little boy or girl to play with," the elephant said.

"Me too!" Little Ted said, sitting up straight and smiling now at everyone who came to the table. A nice old lady bought the elephant for her grandson.

"Bye, bye," the elephant said, waving from the bag that she put him in, "and good luck!"

All afternoon things were bought off Little Ted's stall. Everything except Little Ted.

"Maybe no-one wants an old bear like me," thought Little Ted, getting worried. He barely noticed the little fingers reaching out for him as two little hands came up to the table top.

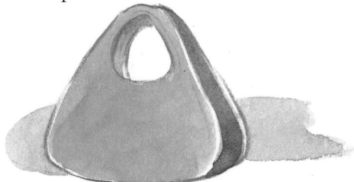

The little hands belonged to a boy who lifted Little Ted down and stared at him for a long time. Little Ted was so surprised that he forgot to smile and just stared back. Then, slowly, the boy began to smile, then Little Ted began to smile and soon they were both grinning from ear to ear.

"He likes me! He likes me! Oh please let him buy me," Little Ted wished as the boy looked at him once more.

"That will be fifty pence please," said the stallholder to the boy.

"But I have not got that much!" the boy replied.

"Oh, he'll never want me now," thought Little Ted. The boy stopped smiling and looked sad as he started to walk away from the stall.

The boy stopped and turned round to the stallholder who looked at the little boy and then at Little Ted. It was late and all the other stalls were packing up. It was time to go home.

"Well, I suppose this bear is a bit old for fifty pence. How much money have you got?"

"Not enough," said the boy sadly, counting his pennies out on to the table.

"I think that just might be enough for an old bear like this," said the stallholder to the boy.

"Thank you!" grinned the boy as he stuffed Little Ted into his backpack and ran over to the door where his mum was waiting for him.

"What have you got there?" she asked.

"My new teddy bear," the boy said proudly.

The boy took Little Ted home and pulled him out of his bag. "We'll have lots of fun together, just you and me," said the boy with a big grin. "And we'll start right now."

Then off they went to play. Little Ted went everywhere with him, joining in all the games, having some tea and getting a bit splashed when he almost fell in the bath. Then, in his pyjamas and very sleepy, the boy took Little Ted upstairs to bed. Snuggling under the covers he was soon fast asleep with Little Ted beside him. As night fell, the stars came out and shone through the bedroom window. Little Ted saw the same twinkling star he had wished on.

"Thank you, star," Little Ted smiled, "for giving me a friend to play with and making my wish come true."

THE SNOWBEAR

THE SNOWBEAR

It was a cold winter's day and all the toys were grumbling. They were bored sitting in the bedroom and could not think of anything to do. Teddy was by the window looking out at the white garden. He had never seen snow before.

The children from the house had been out in the garden earlier and built a snowman.

"I wonder who that is down there," said Teddy.

"That's Mr Snowman," giggled the rag doll. All the other toys had seen snow before and knew all about snowmen. "Let's go down and say 'Hello!'" she chuckled.

"OK," replied Teddy and off they went to put on their coats, as it was very cold outside.

As they walked out on to the snow it crunched underfoot. Teddy looked at it with amazement. It was so soft and white and when it landed on his paw it melted away. "How odd," thought Teddy.

"Come on!" called the rag doll as she got to the snowman first.

Teddy soon caught up with her and said to the snowman in his most polite voice, "Good afternoon, Mr Snowman!" but the snowman did not reply.

Teddy nudged the rag doll and whispered to her, "He seems very rude. He did not say 'Hello!' back."

"He isn't real, Teddy," she giggled. "He is made out of snow. Here, look!" she said as she patted the snowman's side.

"Gosh!" said Teddy in surprise.

"Now we can have some fun," laughed the hippo as he made a snowball and threw it at Teddy.

"Oh!" cried Teddy. "What was that for?"

"Silly Teddy! Now you make one and throw it at me if you can," said the hippo as he ran off.

"Well," thought Teddy, "it didn't hurt." So, off he went after him.

All the toys started making them and soon snowballs were flying everywhere. It was such fun slipping and sliding in the snow: ducking and diving away from the snowballs whizzing about: hiding behind the garden shed and leaping out to catch someone.

Teddy was hit and fell laughing on the soft snow.

"I never thought this would be such fun!" he cried.

"What's this?" Teddy asked the rag doll as he landed next to the sledge the children had left in the garden that morning.

"That's a sledge," she said. "We can have fun riding on it."

All the toys took turns having a ride as they pushed the sledge around the snowy garden. They found a little slope near the garden shed where they could make it go even faster. Soon the slope became very slippery as they scooted up and down.

"Faster! Faster!" shouted Teddy when it was his turn to have a ride. The toys pushed as hard as they could and the sledge went so fast they had to let go.

Teddy whizzed down the icy slope and landed with a thump against the shed wall.

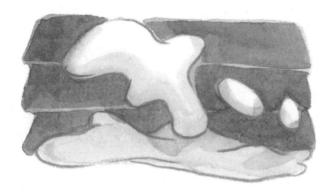

Teddy got up and dusted the snow from his coat.

"That was great!" he yelled but then he heard a soft rumbling sound. "What's that?" he cried.

The snow on the shed roof slid right off and landed on Teddy, covering him from head to paw! He tried to move but could not even wriggle.

"Help! Help!" he shouted from inside the snow.

The toys ran over to see what the noise was.

"Who has made this wonderful snowbear?" they cried.

"It's not a snowbear: it's me!" shouted Teddy through the snow. "Get me out, please!"

The helpful toys soon dug him out of the snow and Teddy said to the rag doll, "I don't think I like being a snowbear very much."

"Well, maybe you would like to make a snowbear instead of being one," she replied.

"I think that would be nicer but I don't know how to start," said the little bear.

"Don't worry," called the hippo. "We can make one together."

First they pushed and rolled a snowball round the garden until it was big enough to make the body and then they made a smaller one for the head.

"I'll do the ears," laughed Teddy, crunching the snow on to the snowbear's head. Then they added arms and patted them into the right shape. They used coloured stones for its face and buttons and an old hat and scarf to finish it off. This was the first snowbear Teddy had ever made and it looked splendid.

The day was colder now and, with the snowbear finished, they all went into the house to get warm.

"What fun snow is!" Teddy said as they took off their coats and hung them up. The toys were chattering and laughing as they all went back to the bedroom where it was cosy and warm.

They had had such a good time playing in the snow that they were not bored any more and it was all thanks to Teddy, who had never even seen snow before.

"I think the snowbear looks just like Teddy," said the rag doll, smiling as she turned to the toys, and they all agreed.

Teddy looked out of the window and admired their snowbear standing proudly in the garden.

HIDE AND SEEK

HIDE AND SEEK

One day Teddy and the toys were playing in the garden.

"What shall we do next?" asked the rag doll.

"Football!" shouted the stuffed dog because he liked chasing balls.

"No, let's have a race!" yelled the red motor car.

"What about hide and seek?" said Teddy. "We can all play that."

The toys thought this was a very good idea. They chose the rag doll to be "It" and so she stood by the garden wall and covered her eyes so that she could not see where they were going to hide.

"One… two… three…," she started calling out in a loud voice, as the toys scattered out around the garden to find their hiding places.

"She's not going to find me first," Teddy said to himself as he went into the wood at the end of the garden. "I'm going to find the best place of all!"

Soon Teddy could not see or hear any of the toys. He could not even hear the rag doll counting to twenty before she came looking for them.

"This must be far enough. She will never find me here," Teddy thought as he crawled into an old plant pot at the bottom of a bush.

At first Teddy thought that he was very clever hiding from the rag doll but as the time went on he got a bit worried.

"Surely she will find me soon," he thought, but still the rag doll did not come. Then he heard someone scratching and tapping on the plant pot.

Teddy kept very quiet as the scratching got louder and the furry nose and whiskers of a mouse poked into the pot.

"What are you doing in there?" asked the mouse.

"I'm playing hide and seek," whispered Teddy. "Please be quiet or the rag doll will find me."

The mouse looked at Ted for a moment and said, "I haven't seen anyone but you all afternoon."

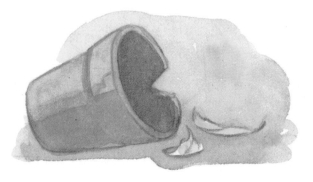

"I thought this game was taking a long time," said Teddy as he crawled out and looked around to see which way to go home. Everything looked different now and he did not know which way to go.

"I must go back home!" he said to the mouse. "Can you help me?"

"I don't know the way," squeaked the mouse, "but my friend might."

They walked along until they came to a large, round, prickly ball. "Here we are," said the mouse.

"But where's your friend?" Teddy asked.

"I'm here," a voice replied.

Ted looked about to see who was there but could not see anyone. Then the mouse laughed saying, "Teddy, this is my friend."

The prickly ball unrolled and there was a hedgehog! Teddy was very surprised and said, "Can you help me get home?"

"I'm afraid I can't," said the hedgehog shaking his head, "but Mrs Blackbird might know."

So off they went to find Mrs Blackbird.

"What is a little bear like you doing here so far from home?" she chirped when they saw her.

"I was playing hide and seek and I'm lost," Teddy said. "Can you help me find my way home?"

"I don't know where your home is but maybe we can find it. Climb up on my back and we will go and look," she said.

Teddy sat on her back and, waving goodbye to Mouse and Hedgehog, they flew up in the air.

Teddy was so excited. He had never been so high before. They were flying over the trees and up into the sky. Down below there were houses and gardens just like his but he still could not see his home. Then he saw the toys in the garden.

"Over there!" Teddy shouted to Mrs Blackbird.

"I can see them too!" she chirped and down they flew.

The toys were amazed as Mrs Blackbird and Teddy landed on the grass.

"Thank you so much for bringing me home, Mrs Blackbird," said Teddy.

"Goodbye, little bear," she sang as she flew away to her home in the woods.

Then Teddy turned around to see his friends again.

"Where have you been?" the rag doll said. "We've been looking everywhere for you. You must have found a really good place to hide."

"I think it was good," Teddy said, "but then I could not find my way home. I thought I might never see you again and that made me sad."

Then Teddy told them all about the mouse and the hedgehog he had met in the woods and how they, and Mrs Blackbird, had helped him to get home.

The toys were amazed when Teddy told them about flying high in the sky.

"I wish we could go flying too," said the rag doll wistfully. "It must be wonderful." And all the other toys agreed with her.

"I know," Teddy said, "let's play a flying game. We can all pretend to be birds like Mrs Blackbird."

With their arms outstretched they ran around the garden "flying" over the grass and swooping around the flower beds until it was time to go in for their tea.

It had been a very exciting afternoon and now Teddy and the toys had an exciting new game to play.

THE LOST KEY

THE LOST KEY

It was a bright spring morning and Teddy and the toys were spring-cleaning the toybox. Lily's mum had already been in this morning to spring-clean her room which was now spick and span and tidier than Teddy had ever seen it before. They all wanted their toybox to be as bright and shiny as the rest of the room.

Just as they were finishing, Teddy heard a very quiet sound. Someone was crying.

"Hush everyone! Listen!" Teddy said. All the toys stopped chattering and now they could all hear someone sobbing. It was coming from the music box. Little Ballerina was sitting in her box weeping into her hanky.

"What's wrong?" asked Teddy.

"Oh, Teddy," cried the little dancer. "I can't find my little golden key. Without it I can't wind up the music box and I won't be able to dance any more without my music. I'm sure it was there last night because I danced for Jack before he went to sleep, but now I can't see it anywhere."

"Dry your tears, Little Ballerina," said Teddy. "We will all help to look for your key, won't we, Toys?"

"Of course we will," they all cried.

They spread out in the bedroom and started to hunt for the key. They looked under the bed and on the shelves, behind the cupboard, where all the little things usually fall, but there was not even a sweet wrapper to be found. Everywhere was so tidy.

"It's not in here," Teddy said to Little Ballerina. "Maybe someone has moved it. I think we are going to have to look outside the bedroom."

The toys went to the door and looked out on to the upstairs landing. There was no-one about upstairs but they could all hear noises coming from the kitchen downstairs. They crept along the hallway to the bathroom. They looked for the little golden key but they could not find it anywhere.

"It's no use," said the hippo miserably. "We'll never find it."

"Don't give up yet," said Teddy, pointing to the laundry basket by the sink. "Maybe it's in there."

The basket was very high and Teddy had to scramble up on to the stool to reach the top of the basket.

Teddy stood on the edge looking down at the clothes. As he leaned over to get a better look at something shiny, there came the sound of footsteps on the stairs. Teddy turned to see who was coming and wobbled over the edge of the basket. Paws outstretched, Teddy fell in and landed with a soft thump on the clothes.

Teddy saw the shiny thing close up now but it was only an old button on a shirt and not the key for the music box. Teddy could not get out of the basket before Lily's mum came into the room and put some more towels into it. Then she took the washing away with Teddy as well!

"I do hope I don't get washed too!" thought Teddy as they went into the kitchen.

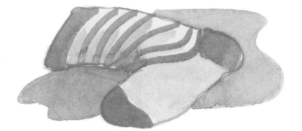

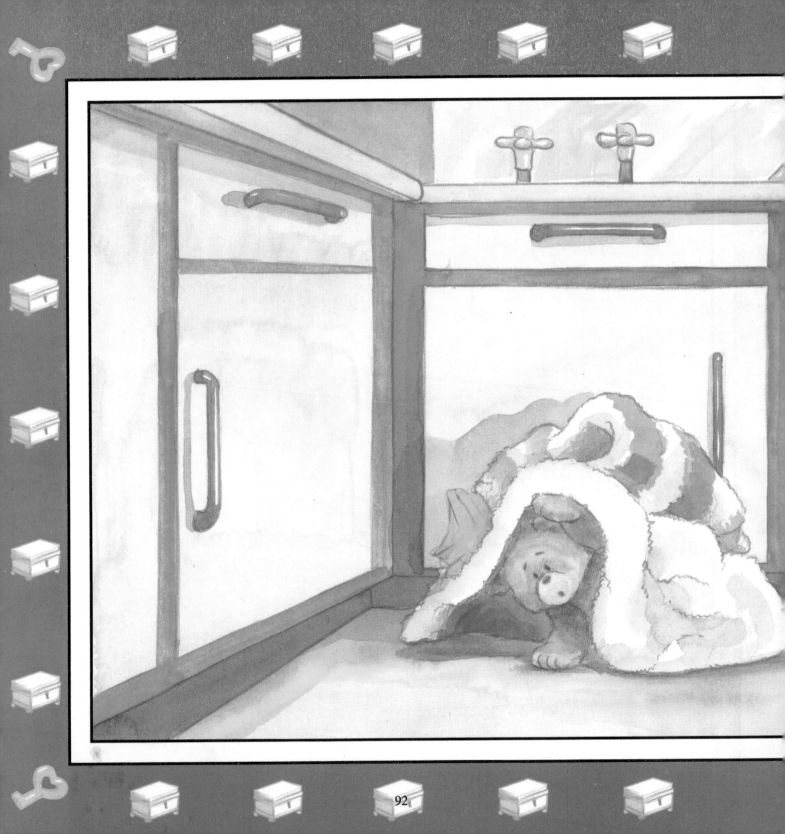

All the laundry from the bathroom, and Teddy, was piled up on the floor ready to be sorted for the washing machine. As Lily's mum shook out the clothes and put them in the machine there was a flash and a tiny tinkling sound as something bounced on the floor.

"What's that?" thought Teddy, scrambling out from under a towel just in time to see the little golden key bounce under the table where it came to a halt. Teddy quickly grabbed the key and held on tight.

"However did you get there?" said Lily's mum in surprise as she spotted Teddy by the table leg. "I think you should be upstairs with all the other toys!" she said, picking Teddy up and putting him on the worktop.

Soon all the laundry was done and piles of sheets and towels and a basket of freshly ironed clothes were ready to go upstairs. Lily's mum put Teddy, still clutching the little key tightly in his paw, on top of the clothes and took the basket up the stairs to Lily's room. As they went into the bedroom all the toys were now sitting gloomily in the toybox.

Teddy winked broadly at them from the top of the basket as he held up his tightly closed paw.

"Look!" cried the hippo to the other toys. "Teddy's come back!"

When Lily's mum had gone, the toys gathered round Teddy to hear his news. Teddy stretched out his paw to Little Ballerina and slowly opened it. There on his outstretched paw was the key.

"Oh, Teddy! You have found it!" she cried. "Quickly, wind up my box so that I can dance again!"

Teddy put the key in and turned it and started the music. Soon the sound of music filled the room and the toys watched as Little Ballerina began to dance.

"Come on," she said as she twirled around happily. "Please join in with me!"

So Teddy and all the toys danced to Little Ballerina's beautiful music, laughing and smiling as they whirled around the floor.

"Thank you so much," said Little Ballerina to the toys when the music ended.

"We have all had such a good time dancing thanks to you," said the toys when the music stopped. Then the tired toys climbed into the toy box and fell fast asleep.

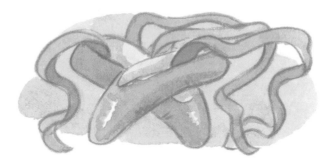

TEDDY'S
NEW FRIEND

TEDDY'S NEW FRIEND

It was very early one morning and everyone was asleep when Teddy first met the new puppy. She was looking around her new home and scampered noisily into the room where he was.

"Who's making all that noise?" groaned Teddy sleepily as he woke up from his wonderful dream about a picnic. "It's too early for anyone to be out of bed yet." He moaned as he rubbed his eyes and opened them slowly. There in front of him two big brown eyes were staring at him! "Who are you? What do you want?" he said grumpily.

"Come and play with me!" the puppy woofed.

"No!" growled Teddy as he tried to go back to sleep. "It's too early for that."

"Oh, come on!" yapped the puppy.

"Hush!" whispered Teddy crossly. "You'll wake everyone up!"

"They can come and play too!" woofed the little puppy and with that she picked Teddy up and trotted off. "Of course Teddy wants to play," she thought. "Everyone wants to play."

Poor Teddy wriggled and jiggled but the puppy would not put him down.

"She has to let go soon," thought Teddy as he was carried through the house. They stopped in the kitchen where the puppy could smell dog biscuits in her bowl. She put Teddy down as she ate them.

"These are great," she said. "Do you want some?"

"No thank you. Teddy bears don't eat dog biscuits," he said as he slowly started to sneak away. Too late! Teddy was not fast enough.

"My red ball is out in the garden," woofed the puppy as she dragged Teddy through the cat flap in the kitchen door. "We can play with that."

Off they went again, this time to look for the ball, but the puppy could not remember where she had left it.

"We'll just look over here," she said as she tramped across the flower bed.

"Oh no!" shouted Teddy. "Look out! You have squashed all those lovely flowers!"

"Well, I didn't mean to," said the puppy. "I was just looking for my ball."

And with that she went to look somewhere else. She got very excited as she rooted around the garden looking here and there. There were so many new smells and things to see.

Teddy followed along, trying to see where she was going.

"I didn't know there were so many things in this garden," Teddy panted because the puppy was going so fast. He followed her to the greenhouse and the compost heap, then across the grass where the washing was drying, then over towards the garden wall but they still could not find her ball. He could see her climbing up over some old flower- pots and trays and on to the top of the wall.

"Your ball won't be up there!" shouted Teddy.

"Well it might be!" she woofed back.

"Come down before you fall!" Teddy said crossly.

"I'm OK," she woofed as she missed her step and tumbled off the wall. Teddy rushed over and caught her just in time.

She landed right on top of Teddy.

"You weigh a lot for a little dog," said Teddy as he stood up and dusted himself off but she took no notice of him as she spotted something in the pond.

"Maybe that's my ball!" she said, running off.

"Oh no! Not again!" moaned Teddy as he ran off after her.

"This is not my ball," barked the puppy, "but it is red." She came out of the pond and dropped an old soggy paper cup on the grass. Then she shook and shook and shook and all the water on her coat flew off making Teddy very wet as he stood next to her.

"You naughty puppy!" Teddy scolded. "Look what you have done!"

The puppy stopped shaking her fur and looked very sad.

"I only wanted to play with you," she said miserably, "and I can't find my ball anywhere."

Teddy started to feel sorry for the little dog. She was only a puppy after all and she did not mean to do any harm. "Oh well," said Teddy kindly, "never mind. We can soon get cleaned up and dried off. Come on, let's go inside now and we will look for your ball later."

"Yes, I'd like that," the little puppy said, and off they went back towards the house. They crept in very quietly through the cat flap because no-one else was awake yet.

Soon they were dry and Teddy gave the little puppy's coat a good brushing to get her clean. Then they wandered across the kitchen to her basket.

"We can look for your ball later when everyone gets up. It is still very early and I would like to sit down for a moment after all that running around," yawned Teddy as they climbed into her basket.

"Well, I suppose we could, just for a moment," yawned the puppy in reply. As she pulled her blanket closer she uncovered her ball.

"So that's where I left it!" she woofed in surprise. "We can play now but let's just have a nap first." They both yawned once more and settled down on the blanket.

A little while later everyone was surprised to see Teddy and the puppy asleep in her basket.

"Wake up, you sleepyheads!" they said, but Teddy and the puppy just yawned and went back to sleep.

WASHING DAY

WASHING DAY

It was Monday and Teddy was helping Sam to do the laundry. Watching washing going round, and soap suds splashing against the glass door of the washing machine, Teddy said, "I'm getting dizzy."

"Don't be silly," said Sam. "You don't have to sit there and watch it. You can help me hang out the clean clothes when they are done later."

Teddy waited, then waited a bit more, because the machine took a lot longer to finish than the little bear expected. At last the washing was ready. They loaded up the big basket with clean clothes and Teddy carried the pegs in the little basket. Outside, the garden was bright and breezy.

"This is a good day to get everything dry," said Sam.

As they pegged the clothes out on the washing line, the breeze got breezier. It was getting harder now to peg out the washing, especially the big things. The wind got stronger and started to push Teddy about.

"Be careful there," Sam said. "We don't want anything to blow away."

"Of course I'll be careful," replied Teddy as the last piece of washing was pegged on the line. "See! It's all done."

Just then a big gust of wind pulled a towel off the line. As more things came loose and the pegs flew off, Teddy grabbed the washing that was flying up in the air.

"Sam! Help me!" Teddy shouted. But Sam had already gone inside the house and did not hear him.

Teddy tried to hold on to the laundry to stop it flying away. The big towel billowed up like a balloon and carried Teddy up into the air!

"Help! Help!" cried Teddy. "Get me down!" But no help came. Up over the washing line Teddy flew, higher and higher. The clothes were flying up into the air all around and soon the garden seemed far away. Teddy looked down.

"Well, I suppose this isn't so bad," thought the little bear. "But I really would like to get down soon."

The wind was quite steady now and Teddy and the towel carried on sailing across the sky. He looked down and could see all the houses in his street and from each washing line more clothes were flying up towards him.

There were socks and shirts, trousers and dresses flying around in the sky with Teddy and his towel. At last the wind dropped a little and the little bear landed on the weather-vane on top of the tallest house in his street.

"Thank goodness!" said Teddy as he sat down on the weather-vane. "Now I can get down."

Then the wind blew again and spun Teddy and the weather-vane around throwing Teddy up into the air.

"Oh no! Not again!" yelled Teddy as he sailed across the sky once more. He caught hold of the TV aerial as he passed the chimney of the next house. He crept along the roof towards the end of the house but it was no use. The wind was stronger now and whisked Teddy into the air again.

There was lots of washing from all the houses up in the air with Teddy. He reached out at anything that was going past and caught hold of a pillowcase that filled up like a parachute.

Then Teddy had a bright idea. "Just a minute!" he laughed. "I know how I can get down."

Holding on to the pillowcase, he started to grab anything that was flying past.

"I'm sure that one must be ours, and that one, and that one," he said.

Each time he caught something he got a little heavier and dropped down a little bit lower. Soon Teddy had a big pile of clothes and all sorts of washing in his arms as he sailed gently down to his garden.

131

He landed in a big heap with all the washing on the grass.

"I mustn't let Sam know I lost all the washing," said Teddy. Quickly he ran around the garden and picked up all the pegs. Then, using the big basket to stand on, he pegged out all the washing on the line once more. It was such a windy day that everything was almost dry.

Teddy was feeling proud of himself for sorting out the laundry and putting it safely on the line.

"I don't think anyone will know it hasn't been there all along," Teddy thought, smiling to himself. "I think I'll just sit down and have a rest because it's been a very busy morning." He sat and watched the washing blowing on the line, feeling very pleased with himself.

Sam came out of the house to find Teddy.

"Have you been waiting for that washing to dry all this time?" Sam asked Teddy. Teddy just smiled.

"I think it might be dry enough to take in now," said Sam, feeling the clothes on the line. Sam and Teddy started to take the washing down and put it in the basket.

"That's odd," Sam said, looking at Teddy. "I don't remember these socks and where did this skirt come from? And these trousers. I'm sure they aren't ours."

Sam was very surprised when Teddy told him all about his adventure on this very windy day.

"What a clever little bear you are," Sam said, and off they went to find their washing and give everyone else theirs back in return.

CAPTAIN TEDDY

CAPTAIN TEDDY

It was a hot, sunny, summer's day. Teddy and Penguin were sitting under the old oak tree feeling very left out. They could hear the children playing with their boats down by the stream.

"When are we going to get a turn to play?" grumbled Teddy to Penguin.

"I don't know. I hope it's soon," replied Penguin.

The children came back to the tree to have their sandwiches. Afterwards, they chatted on the grass.

"I don't want to spend all afternoon sitting under a tree," complained Teddy to Penguin.

"Me neither," replied Penguin.

Teddy got up and looked at the children, who were still talking. "Let's go and play," said Teddy.

As soon as they were away from the children, they ran across the grass to the stream. The children had tied the toy boats to the bank with string and there they bobbed up and down on the water in the warm breeze.

"Let's go aboard and have some fun. We can play pirates," giggled Teddy. "Ahoy there, Penguin!" Teddy called, jumping on to the biggest boat.

"Ahoy there, Captain Teddy!" laughed Penguin, climbing aboard. They walked across the deck of the boat, grinning from ear to ear. It rocked beneath them but they did not mind because it was fun to be pirates.

"Cast off!" commanded Teddy as they untied the boat. It swung out into the stream and their pirate ship was ready to sail away.

Captain Teddy stood proudly on deck keeping a look out and Penguin steered the boat. They were in the middle of the stream now and the water was getting faster. The sail billowed out as the strong breeze blew them along.

It was a very fine day for sailing.

"Look out! Sea monsters!" shouted Teddy as the ducklings swam out of the way of their boat.

"Sea monsters indeed!" Penguin laughed when he saw them. They sailed on in the hot sunshine and as they did the stream got wider and deeper. All the little fishes watched them as they bobbed along in their boat in the water above.

Down below in the deep water, a big fish thought it would take a look too.

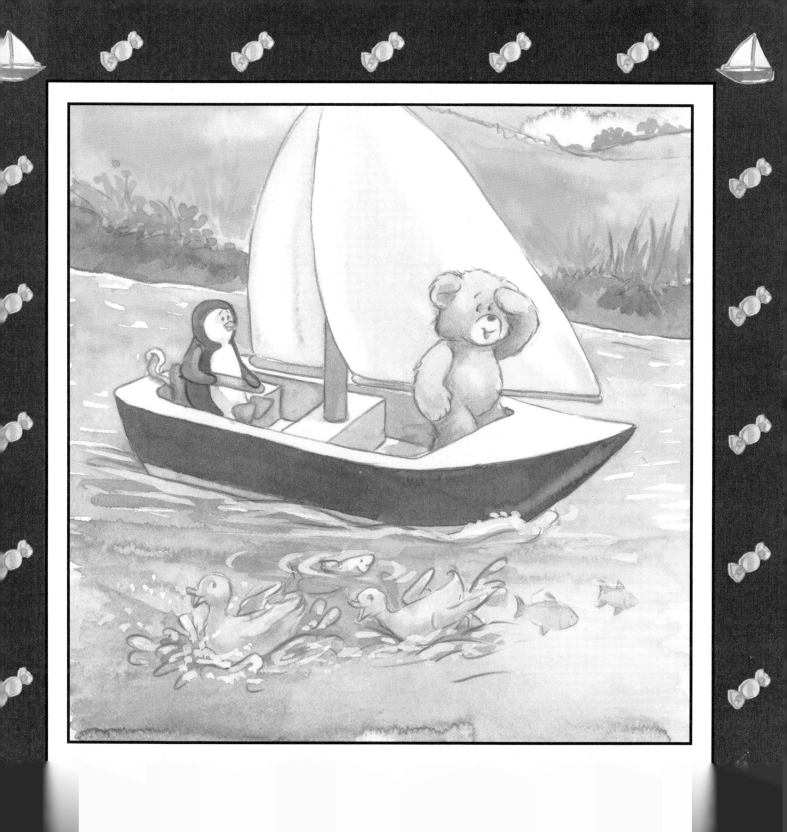

The big fish swam up towards the boat. Teddy saw it coming and cried, "Help! A sea monster!"

"Not again!" grinned Penguin.

"It's true this time!" shouted Teddy, but it was too late. The big fish swam faster and faster and jumped right out of the water and over their boat, making great big waves which splashed everywhere. The boat rocked so much that Teddy and Penguin were thrown about and the mast fell down.

"Abandon ship!" cried Captain Teddy. Penguin and Teddy scrambled off their boat and on to a little island in the middle of the stream. They watched the boat go crashing along in the water. On and on down the stream until it was out of sight.

"Gosh, Teddy!" Penguin said. "We've been shipwrecked."

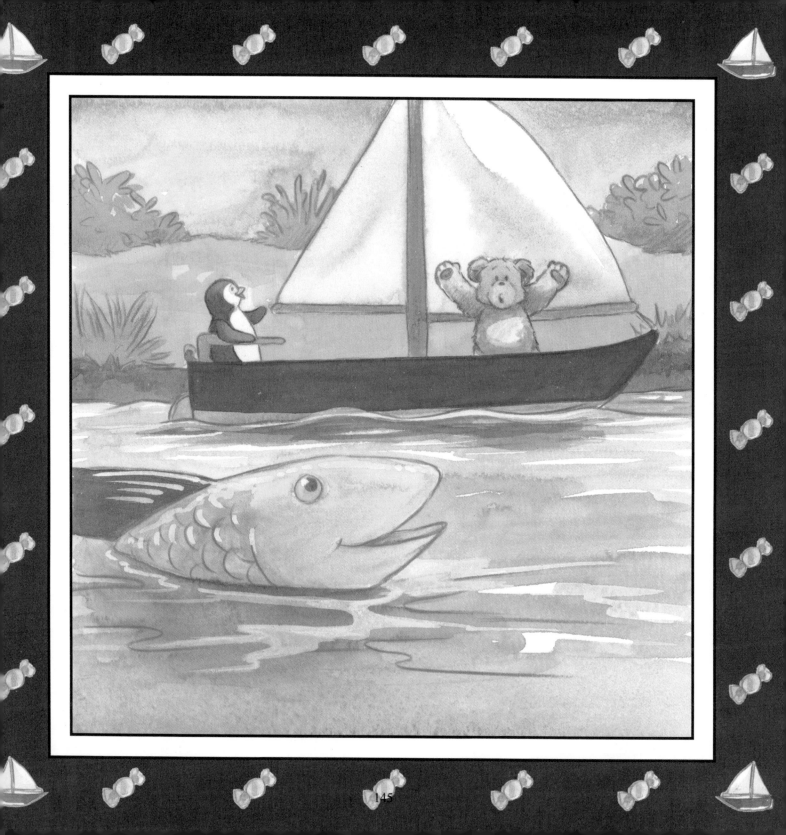

They looked around them and Teddy said, "Penguin, I think this must be a treasure island."

"Do you really think so?" replied Penguin.

"I'm sure it is," said Teddy boldly. "Let's go and look for treasure."

Over the rocks and under the bushes and in the grass they looked. All over the island they hunted for treasure and just as they were about to give up Penguin saw something glittering on the ground.

"Teddy! Come on over here!" shouted Penguin excitedly. Teddy ran over to him, eager to see what Penguin had found but it was just an old bottle top.

"Oh bother! That's not treasure," Teddy said sadly. "But wait, what's that over there?"

There was something else sticking out of the grass.

They pulled and tugged at it until at last Teddy could see what it was.

"Is it gold, or diamonds, or rubies?" asked Penguin excitedly.

"No, it's just a plastic box," sighed Teddy. "It isn't treasure at all."

"But what's inside it?" asked Penguin.

"I don't know," replied Teddy, "but I suppose it wouldn't hurt to have a look."

They opened the box and saw lots of sweets in rainbow colours. Teddy's eyes lit up with delight.

"This is real treasure after all!" They were so pleased with their treasure that they laughed and whooped and jumped up and down with joy.

"This is much better than gold or diamonds," agreed Penguin.

They picked up the box and carried it carefully across the stepping stones to the bank of the stream. As they walked back to the children and the old oak tree, Teddy said to Penguin,

"How do you think the treasure got there?"

"I don't know, but the children might," replied Penguin.

Back at the tree the two friends sat down quietly with their treasure safely between them. It had been a very exciting afternoon and all they wanted to do now was sit for a while. The children were still talking and had not noticed they had gone at all.

Then one of the children said, "Let's go and play pirates."

They all thought this was a very good idea for Teddy and Penguin too. "Oh no! Not again!" groaned Teddy. Penguin just laughed and laughed.

TEDDY'S SURPRISE

TEDDY'S SURPRISE

Ohhhh!" Teddy yawned, stretching out two furry paws as he woke up. "I'm sure this is going to be a brilliant day," Teddy said to himself. "After all it is my birthday. I wonder how many cards I'll get? Maybe I'll get some presents and a huge cake."

Teddy was so excited he could not wait to see all the other toys today but where were they? Teddy could not see any of the other toys around him so he climbed down out of the toy cupboard in the playroom to go and find them.

"They must have got up early," he thought as he jumped off the last shelf and on to the carpet. "I wonder if they have gone to fetch my presents."

Teddy skipped along to where he met the rag doll.

"Good morning, Ragdoll," Teddy said cheerfully.

"Good morning to you too," replied the rag doll with a smile.

"You are up very early today, Ragdoll. Did you get up for something special?" Teddy smiled back.

"Yes," answered the rag doll. "But I can't remember what it was."

"Maybe you had to make a cake?" Teddy said.

"No, that's not it," said the rag doll shaking her head. "But I'm sure it was something to do with a kitchen." Then she smiled at Teddy and said, "Now I remember! I have to spring-clean the kitchen in the dolls' house. Thank you very much, Teddy, for reminding me. Bye! Bye!" Then off went the rag doll with her brush and bucket.

"Oh dear," thought Teddy sadly. "Ragdoll didn't remember my birthday at all." Teddy walked along not quite as happy as before.

Then he saw Hippo pulling out paper and crayons from a box.

"What are you doing, Hippo? Are you making anything special for someone?"

"Me? No, I don't think so," replied Hippo. "I wish I could remember what I was supposed to do today."

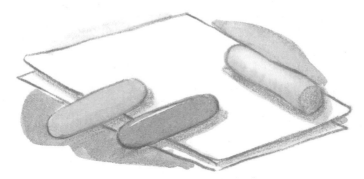

"Maybe you have to write a letter or make a card for someone special?" said Teddy helpfully.

"No, that's not it but I know it's something to do with writing," replied Hippo. "Wait a minute! I remember! I have to help the little toys learn to write their alphabet. Thank you, Teddy, for helping me remember." And with that Hippo hurried away.

As Teddy walked along the little stuffed dog ran past him.

"Wait!" called Teddy. "Where are you going in such a rush?"

"I have to go and fetch something."

"What are you going for?" asked Teddy. "Is it something nice? A present perhaps?"

"No, I don't think it's a present. But it is nice," woofed the little dog. "Now I remember. It's that bone I left in the garden."

Just then Clown drove past in his car. "I have to fetch my bone," barked the little stuffed dog.

"Hop in and I'll take you," laughed Clown.

"Oh thank you, Clown," said the stuffed dog, getting into Clown's car. "And thank you too, Teddy, for helping me to remember my bone."

"Bye! Bye!" they said, driving off.

Clown and the little stuffed dog soon drove out of sight and Teddy was left standing all alone once more.

"Everyone is so busy today," sighed Teddy. "No-one has remembered my birthday. I haven't got a cake or a card or a present," said Teddy, who was now feeling very sorry for himself. "I suppose I may as well go back to the toy cupboard on my own. There is nothing else to do and everyone is too busy even to play with me."

Then the sad little bear walked slowly back to the playroom. Teddy walked with his head down, not looking where he was going, and bumped into the playroom door, which was shut.

"That's odd," Teddy thought. "I don't remember closing this door."

Teddy pushed the door open and suddenly there was lots of noise. Teddy jumped back in surprise.

"Happy birthday, Teddy! Happy birthday!" shouted all the toys together. There were streamers and balloons filling the air all around him.

"You did remember my birthday after all!" Teddy grinned at them.

"Of course we did!" laughed the rag doll. "But it was hard pretending that we didn't remember your birthday. It would have spoiled the surprise."

As well as the balloons there was a beautiful big card from them which Hippo had made with the paper and crayons. The little stuffed dog and Clown had gone to fetch the presents and not the little dog's bone and, last but not least, Ragdoll had made a delicious birthday cake with candles.

They all had lots of fun playing Pass the Parcel and Musical Chairs and lots of other games and everyone had a wonderful time. When it was time to stop, Teddy said, "Thank you everyone for a great party and for being such good friends."

Then Hippo shouted, "Three cheers for Teddy!"

"Hip, hip, hurray! Hip, hip, hurray! Hip, hip, hurray!" cheered the toys as they all gave Teddy a great big birthday hug.

They helped to tidy up when the party was over and soon it was time to go to sleep.

"That was the best birthday I ever had," smiled Teddy to himself later, yawning and stretching as he settled down to sleep. "I have such good friends. I hope they forget my birthday again next year."

THE VISITOR

THE VISITOR

Today was a very special day because visitors were coming to tea. Teddy helped with the dusting and the polishing and the house was clean and shiny. Everyone was waiting, ready for their visitors.

Ding! Dong! The doorbell rang.

"They are here!" shouted Teddy excitedly. The visitors had brought a baby with them and Teddy was allowed to sit right next to it on the sofa.

"Hello, Baby," smiled Teddy.

"Gurgle, gurgle," replied the baby, pulling at Teddy's fur.

"Stop that! It tickles!" laughed Teddy as the baby wriggled down off the sofa and on to the floor. "Wait a minute, Baby! Come back here!" called Teddy but the baby did not stop.

"Excuse me!" said Teddy to Susie, Teddy's little girl. "The baby's got off the sofa and is getting away!"

"Not now, Teddy," she said. She was too busy chatting to the visitors to listen to Teddy properly.

"I suppose I had better go and look after it before it gets into trouble," thought Teddy and went off to find the baby. The baby had found some chocolate and now there were bits of chocolate wrapper on the floor and sticky finger marks on the clean wall as well.

"Oh dear! Stop, Baby! Stop!" cried Teddy, running to catch up.

"Gurgle, gurgle," giggled the baby as it toddled off again. Teddy saw the chocolate-covered baby go into the playroom.

Sitting tidily on the shelf in the playroom were the pots of paint, paper and crayons which the children had been playing with earlier. The baby thought these would be great fun and pulled the paint off the shelf splashing it everywhere, making messy baby pictures. Next the baby pulled down the box of crayons, spilling them all over the floor, and started to make even messier squiggles on the wall.

"Don't do that!" cried Teddy. "You're making such a mess!"

But the baby just giggled and said, "Gurgle, gurgle!" and toddled off once more.

"How can such a small child make such a big mess?" thought Teddy as he scurried around after the baby, trying to tidy everything up, but he still was not fast enough.

As Teddy chased after it, the baby wandered off into Susie's room. It pulled the big fluffy pillows off the bed and began jumping on them. The baby was very good at jumping and laughed and giggled as it bounced higher and higher. Just as Teddy caught up to the baby it made a great big jump and one of the pillows burst! Teddy and the baby both tumbled on to the pillows as the feathers flew up into the air.

"Got you!" laughed Teddy as the feathers swirled around. Teddy and the baby danced around as the feathers flew about, tickling them as they fell.

"It's time to stop now, Baby," said Teddy, holding the baby's hand. "But I think I will have to clean you up first before anyone sees the mess you are in."

Teddy and the baby were covered in paint and feathers as he took the baby by the hand and went into the bathroom.

"Come on," laughed Teddy. "It's time to get cleaned up."

"Gurgle, gurgle," giggled the baby. The baby was very good for Teddy as he washed all the paint and chocolate off its face and hands. Then Teddy brushed the feathers from the baby's clothes and combed the little child's hair.

"There!" said Teddy, smiling at the baby, who was now all clean and tidy. "You would never know you had been in such a mess. I think it's time to take you back." Then, holding hands, Teddy and the baby left the bathroom to go back to the living room where the rest of the visitors were.

As they walked back to the sofa, Teddy saw all the mess that the baby had made.

"Never mind, Baby, I'll clean it up for you," said Teddy. "But first we must get you back on the sofa."

In the living room everyone was still chatting as Teddy helped Baby to climb back on the sofa.

"Now just you wait here while I clean up that mess," Teddy smiled. The clean and tidy baby was a bit tired now and sat on the sofa and had a little nap.

Teddy slipped away and started to clean up the mess the baby had made. Soon the sticky chocolate marks and the messy paint were washed off the walls and Teddy collected all the feathers and stuffed them back into the pillow.

He looked around to see that all was tidy again.

"I think that will do," thought Teddy. "If I go back now no-one will know there has been any mess." And off he went back to the living room and climbed up on the sofa next to the baby.

Then Susie came up to Teddy and said, "Hello, Teddy. Now what did you want to tell me?" She was looking at Teddy in surprise.

"Oh, it was nothing," said Teddy, puzzled.

"But, Teddy," Susie said, "how did you get into such a mess?"

"What mess?" said Teddy. He had been so busy cleaning up after the baby that he had forgotten to clean himself! He looked at his paint-covered paws and said, "Oh! That mess!" And he laughed and told Susie all about the very messy baby.

THE RUNAWAY TRAIN

THE RUNAWAY TRAIN

Today Teddy was wandering through the streets of a model village. All the houses and shops and gardens were very small. They were so small that Teddy felt like a giant walking down the streets.

"There must be very little people living here," he chuckled as he looked through one of the windows but there were only model figures inside.

This village was perfect. It had roads, everything, even tiny model ducks on the pond. Teddy's favourite thing was the train, which had its own train station. It was great fun.

"I would love to go for a train ride today," thought Teddy. "I wonder what time the next one goes?" And off he went to the station to find out.

The little train was standing at the station. It had just pulled in and all the passengers had got off. The train driver was checking the engine and making sure that everything was ready for the next train ride.

As Teddy walked on to the station platform, the train driver put up a notice which said, 'The next train ride will be at three o'clock.' Then he went off to have a cup of tea.

Teddy looked at the big clock on the station wall to see what time it was. It said a quarter to three.

"That's only fifteen minutes to wait. That's not very long," thought Teddy so he sat down and waited for the driver to come back.

As he sat there Teddy saw Squirrel jump on to the train.

He jumped and scampered all over the train. "Hey you!" cried Teddy. "What are you doing there?"

"It's none of your business," replied Squirrel cheekily and started to jump about looking at all the levers and handles in the train's cab.

"Come out! It's dangerous to play in there!" shouted Teddy, running over to the train.

"Look at me!" laughed Squirrel. "I'm driving the train!"

The silly animal would not stop pretending to drive the train. Before Teddy could reach him Squirrel had pulled the levers and suddenly a big whoosh of steam billowed out.

Naughty Squirrel jumped off the train in fright. Then the train began to hiss and creak and move out of the station and along the track.

Quick as a flash Teddy ran alongside the train. It was getting faster and faster as it pulled out of the station. Soon Teddy was coming up to the end of the platform. He made the biggest jump he could and landed on the last carriage of the train.

"I must stop the train!" Teddy yelled at the frightened animal. "Quick, go and get help! Now!"

The train was going much faster now. Clickety-clack! Clickety-clack! along the railway track.

Teddy tried pulling and pushing the levers but nothing seemed to slow the train down. It was now racing along through the village and over the bridge.

"Everything is going so fast," thought the worried little bear. "I hope Squirrel can get some help soon."

Squirrel ran off to find the train driver.

"Whatever do you want, Little Squirrel?" the kind train driver asked.

Squirrel was chattering and jumping about so fast that the driver could not understand him. Then he pulled and tugged at the driver, who eventually got up to see what was the matter.

"Oh dear me!" the train driver cried when he saw that his train was missing. "Where's my lovely train?"

When he saw the little train racing around the village he ran as fast as he could to catch it. He waved his arms up and down as he shouted to Teddy, "Pull the brake! It's the big, red handle!"

"OK!" shouted Teddy back, pulling the big, red handle with all his might.

It was very hard work but, as Teddy tugged and tugged, the handle moved and the train started to slow down. Clickety-clack, clack, clack. Clickety-clack, clack. Clickety-clack went the train as it slowed down. With a big hiss of steam the train came to a stop, right in the middle of the station.

"Well done, Teddy!" said the driver, smiling and giving Teddy a big pat on the back. "You have saved the train and I think you will make a fine train driver yourself one day!"

Teddy climbed off the train and went over to see the squirrel. "Thank you for getting help, Squirrel," said Teddy.

"That's all right," replied Squirrel, as he turned and walked sadly away. "I'm sorry for being so silly."

"Hold on, wait!" called out Teddy. "I know you didn't mean to start the train and you won't do it again. And you did go and get help so you don't have to go away."

Then the train driver came up to them and said, "You have both been very brave today. Would you like to have a proper train ride now as a reward?"

"Oh yes please!" they both said together. "But please, Mr Driver," asked Teddy, "can we go a bit slower this time?"

"Of course we can," the train driver laughed as he climbed aboard.

Teddy and Squirrel took their seats in the carriage and the train pulled out of the station once more. They had a lovely ride around the village and this time they enjoyed it very much.

THE PRIZE

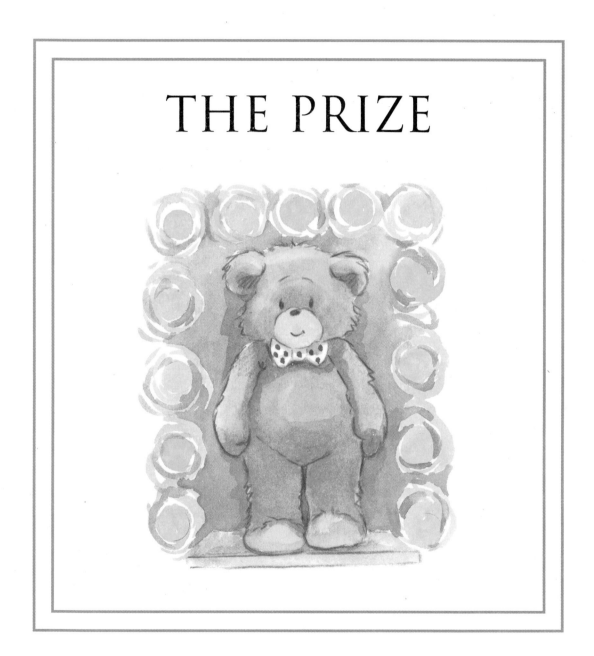

THE PRIZE

It was opening time again at the funfair and Teddy waited for the music to begin and the coloured lights to go on. Teddy, you see, was a prize on a stall at the funfair. Every day he stood on the shelf with the other prizes waiting to be won and because he was the top prize no-one had won him yet.

On Teddy's stall you had to catch the plastic ducks which swam round and round. It was very hard and you had to catch three ducks to win Teddy. As long as Teddy had been there no-one had caught three ducks.

"I do hope someone will win me today," said Teddy to the goldfish.

"And me too!" wiggled the goldfish.

Soon there were lots of people laughing and jostling as they came into the fair. There were all sorts of people going for rides and playing games. Many of them came to Teddy's stall but none of them won Teddy.

Then out of the corner of his eye he saw a little girl come towards him.

She paid the lady at the stall and got her fishing pole to try and catch some ducks.

At first Teddy did not take much notice of her. She had to concentrate very hard as the ducks swam by so quickly. Then, much to Teddy's surprise, she caught a duck.

"I never thought she would catch even one," said Teddy to himself and he began to watch her more closely.

The little girl did it again!

"She's caught another one!" whispered Teddy to the goldfish. "But I bet she'll never get three. No-one ever gets three!" The goldfish wiggled its tail back at Teddy in agreement. The little girl was concentrating very hard now.

"Come on, you can do it!" whispered Teddy.

Slowly and very carefully she tried again. She hooked another duck! That made three and she grinned at Teddy as the lady on the stall said,

"Well done! You have won the teddy bear!" as she handed Teddy to the delighted little girl.

"Oh, Teddy," she said, "we are going to have lots of fun together." And she gave him a big hug.

"Goodbye, goldfish!" waved Teddy as they left the stall.

Teddy was so excited. All this time he had watched the people going on rides and having fun but had never had a turn himself.

"What shall we do first?" asked the little girl. "Would you like to go on the dodgem cars?"

"Oh yes please!" said Teddy, who was thrilled that he was going on his first ride.

They sat in the bright red car and bumped and skidded across the floor knocking into the other cars.

Teddy was quite puffed out when they finished, he had been laughing so much. They went on the roundabout next and then on to the little girl's favourite ride of all, the swing boats. Teddy decided that he liked the swings best too and so now this was Teddy's favourite as well!

Soon their turn on the swings was over and they went to look for something else to do.

"What's that lovely smell?" asked Teddy as they walked through the fair.

"Come on! I'll show you!" the little girl replied. She took Teddy's paw and they went over to the sweet stall. There were toffee-apples and doughnuts, sticks of rock and lollipops and, best of all, there was fluffy, pink, candy floss.

"Oh, please can we have some of that?" Teddy said excitedly.

They bought some candy floss and it was delicious. Then they walked through the fair and the music played loudly and fast and the bright lights flashed and everyone looked very happy.

"I wish this day would never end," smiled Teddy.

The next stall was where Teddy had come from. There they waited for the little girl's parents to come over to them. Then she smiled and, holding Teddy out in front of her, she said to them,

"Look what I've won! Isn't he a wonderful teddy bear?"

"Yes he is," they said. "But we have to go now, it's time to go home."

Teddy looked sad.

"What's wrong, Teddy?" she said to the little bear.

"Well, you are going home now. I won't see you again and I will have to go back on the shelf again."

"But, Teddy," she replied, "you are my prize, you can come home with me!"

"Can I really?" replied Teddy.

"Yes!" said the little girl and they all went out.

"This is your new home, Teddy," she said as she took him to see her room and meet all the other toys.

"This is wonderful. I'm very glad you came to the fair," Teddy said.

"Come on, there's something else I think you will like too," the little girl said and she took him out into the garden. There in the corner was a swing.

"I know it's not as big as the ones at the fair but we can ride on it every day if you like," she said.

"Can we have a go now?" asked Teddy.

"Yes," she laughed and they were soon swinging up into the air.

"I'm very glad I was your prize," Teddy said as they played.

"And I am too," the little girl smiled.

BUBBLES

BUBBLES

Teddy was in a hurry. The rag doll had asked him to come to tea at the dolls' house and it was almost tea-time and he did not want to be late. He really liked going to the dolls' house because the rag doll made such tasty teas.

"I do hope she's made some cake today," thought Teddy as he hurried along. "That's my favourite."

Teddy arrived at the house and knocked loudly on the door.

"Hello, Teddy," said the rag doll as she opened the door. "Come on in. You are just in time for tea."

They sat down to a delicious tea with sandwiches, biscuits and cake, just as Teddy had hoped.

"You do make the best cakes, Ragdoll," Teddy said as he finished the last piece. "I enjoyed that."

Now that they had finished, Ragdoll said, "I'm glad you enjoyed your tea but now we have to clear the table. Remember, Teddy, today it is your turn to help with the washing-up."

"Of course it is. I remember now," Teddy replied, trying to smile.

Then he helped Ragdoll clear the table and carry the dirty dishes into the kitchen.

"Here you are," said the rag doll, handing an apron to Teddy so he would not get wet. "If you carry on with the washing-up I'll go and finish tidying up." And with a smile she left the kitchen.

Teddy turned round to the sink and looked at all the dishes sitting there waiting to be washed.

"Now where do I start?" he thought to himself when the rag doll had gone.

Teddy had not actually done any washing-up before but he had seen the rag doll and other toys do it so he thought he knew what to do. Teddy put on the apron that the rag doll had given him and had a think about what to do next.

"I think I shall have some of this first," he said, putting a big squeeze of washing-up liquid in the sink.

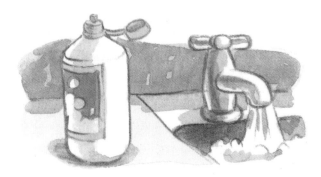

"Next, some water," said Teddy as he turned on the taps. Teddy splashed about and made bubbles in the water for the washing-up. He like making bubbles, it was fun.

Teddy laughed as he made lots of bubbles, which floated up in the air.

"Oh, that one's huge!" he giggled as he turned round and tried to catch it.

The great big bubble was floating away. As Teddy turned round towards the big bubble he knocked over the bottle of washing-up liquid into the water. Then he forgot to turn the taps off. Silly Teddy did not see what he had done as he was too busy laughing and chasing the bubbles. He had forgotten all about the dirty dishes.

Teddy did not see the sink fill up with bubbles. Then bubbles spilled out on to the floor and still they kept on spreading.

Teddy did not notice the huge pile of bubbles behind him. He was far too busy chasing the pretty rainbow coloured ones that were floating out of the kitchen. The shiny bubbles bobbed away in the air, followed by the little teddy bear.

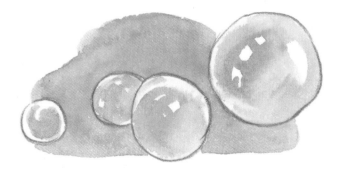

Pop! Pop! went the bubbles as they burst when Teddy touched them. Teddy laughed in surprise.

"I'd better make some more!" he chuckled to himself and he turned round to go back into the kitchen. The little teddy bear was amazed. He had never seen so many bubbles. They filled the kitchen and were coming out of the door.

"Have you finished the dishes yet?" he heard the rag doll call.

"No. Not quite!" replied Teddy, rushing into the kitchen. He slipped and slid as he made his way across the floor towards the sink.

The rag doll came into the kitchen and walked into a sea of foam.

"Whatever is going on?" the rag doll said as she bumped into Teddy in the middle of the bubbles.

Holding hands so that they did not fall on the slippery floor, they both went over to the sink. The rag doll helped Teddy turn off the taps and lift the washing-up bottle out of the sink. Everything was covered in bubbles.

"Come on, Teddy," she said. "We will have to mop all these bubbles up."

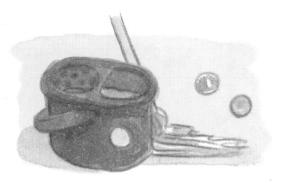

"OK," Teddy grinned sheepishly. They fetched the mop and bucket and got some cloths and started to clean up.

When they had finished all the bubbles were gone off the floor and now it was so clean and shiny with all that mopping that it looked brand new.

Teddy went back to the sink and looked glumly at all the dirty dishes that still had to be washed.

"I'm sorry about not doing the dishes yet," said Teddy sadly. "I forgot all about them."

"That's all right," smiled the rag doll at Teddy. "I'm sure if I help you we can get them done without any bother," she laughed. "After all, with your help we do have a lovely clean kitchen floor now."

Teddy went over to the sink and this time he was very careful and only put a little washing-up liquid in the water and he remembered to turn the taps off.

He still made lots of bubbles in the sink but, of course, this time they were to wash up all the dishes. Ragdoll went to get a tea towel so that she could dry up for Teddy and then they did the dishes together.

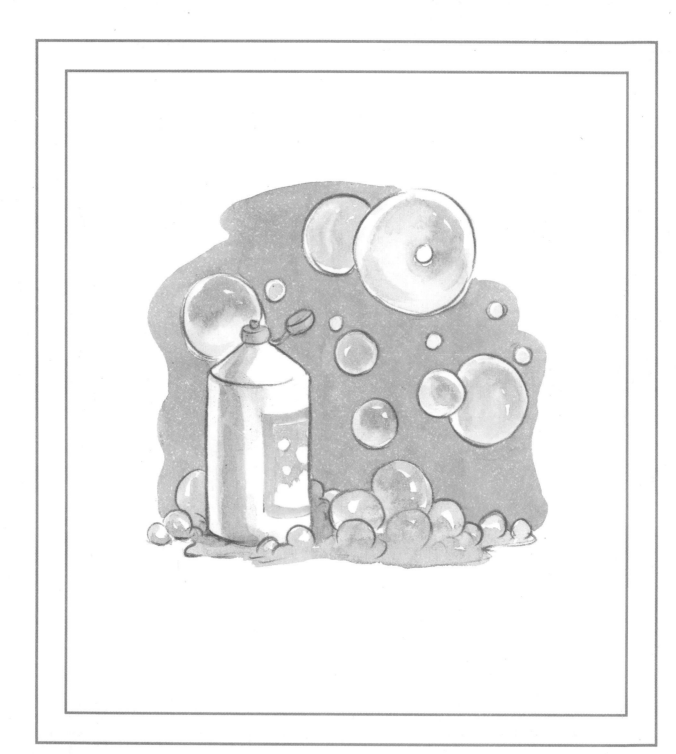

THE GHOST

THE GHOST

All day long the toys had been playing in the garden. All, that is, except the little white rabbit, who had been very cross with everyone because they would not play the game she wanted.

"I want us to play with my ball," Rabbit said.

"No, not now," Teddy said kindly to the rabbit. "We can play your game later but now it's Hippo's turn to choose."

At this, she stamped her feet and shouted, then she picked up her ball and went off to sulk. If she could not have her game she was not going to play with the other toys at all. She was being a very naughty little rabbit indeed.

At last everyone went inside because it was almost time for bed.

Soon the toys were asleep. Teddy was having a lovely dream when someone started to shake him.

"Wake up, Teddy! Wake up, please," whispered the little stuffed dog.

"What?" said Teddy, sleepily. "Is it morning already? I've only just shut my eyes," he yawned.

"No, it's not morning yet," the little dog whispered. "Please wake up. There are some very strange noises coming from over there," the dog said, pointing to the door, "and I'm scared."

When Teddy heard this he woke up properly.

"What sort of noises?" he asked, peering across the room to the door.

"Listen! There it goes again," the little dog said.

"Whooooo! Whooooo!" went the noise outside the door. "Scratch, scratch, scratch!"

The spooky noises were waking up all the toys.

It was dark and the toys were huddled at the foot of the bed trying to be brave. The noises outside the door were getting louder and, when the door opened a bit, they could all see a strange shape floating past.

"Oh my!" squeaked the little stuffed dog. "It's a ghost!" The other toys nodded in agreement.

"A ghost?" whispered Teddy. "Are you sure?"

"Yes!" they all whispered back. "Whatever shall we do now?"

"I think we should go after it and find out what it wants," Teddy said.

"I'm too scared. Can't you go, Teddy?" the little dog asked quietly.

"We'll be all right if we just stick together," replied Teddy, who was also scared. So all the toys crept slowly towards the door.

They went through the door to follow the ghost.

"Whooooo! Whooo! Scritch! Scratch!" The spooky noises were getting louder now as the toys got closer and closer to the ghostly shape.

Teddy peered around the corner of the toy cupboard, hoping that the ghost would not see him and all the other toys as they crept along the landing.

"Boo!" shouted the ghost at Teddy, as it rushed past him and pushed him down to the floor.

"Hey you!" shouted Teddy, jumping to his feet. "You can't go pushing people around even if you are a ghost." He was so annoyed with the ghost that he forgot to be scared and ran after it. He chased the ghost through the house and all the toys followed them.

Teddy got closer and closer. The spooky ghost floated faster and faster away from Teddy and the toys.

"We'll never catch it!" cried the little dog.

"Yes, we will!" shouted Teddy boldly, as he jumped on to the ghost's long tail and grabbed hold of it as hard as he could. The ghost and Teddy fell in a big heap on the floor and rolled around as it tried to escape.

"You're not going to get away from me now!" shouted Teddy as the toys came running up to them. "It's not very nice to scare us in the middle of the night."

All the toys stood and stared at Teddy and the ghost, who were tangled up in a big heap on the floor.

257

The little dog jumped up and switched on the light. Teddy was puzzled. The ghost seemed much smaller than it did when they were running around the house, and when he poked it, it said, "Ouch!"

"You're a funny ghost," Teddy said, looking more closely. It did not look very spooky as it tried to wriggle away. As the ghost pulled and tugged, trying to get away, Teddy saw that he had hold of a big white sheet and underneath was the little white rabbit!

"It's you!" Teddy said in surprise. "You're not a real ghost after all. What do you mean by scaring us and pretending to be a ghost?"

The toys were angry with the rabbit for playing such a nasty trick on them and now the little white rabbit looked scared.

"I'm sorry," said the little rabbit. "I only wanted to scare you a bit. I didn't think you liked me when you wouldn't play my game with me."

"But, Rabbit," said Teddy, "it wasn't your turn to choose the game. You could have played Hippo's game with us if you wanted to. Everyone has to have a turn, that's only fair."

"Oh, I see," replied the rabbit sadly. "I promise I won't be mean again."

The toys felt sorry for the sad little rabbit even though she had been naughty.

"Tomorrow we can all play together again, can't we, Toys?" Teddy said.

"Yes," they all nodded sleepily.

"And now," Teddy said, yawning too, "we should all go back to bed."

THE BELL

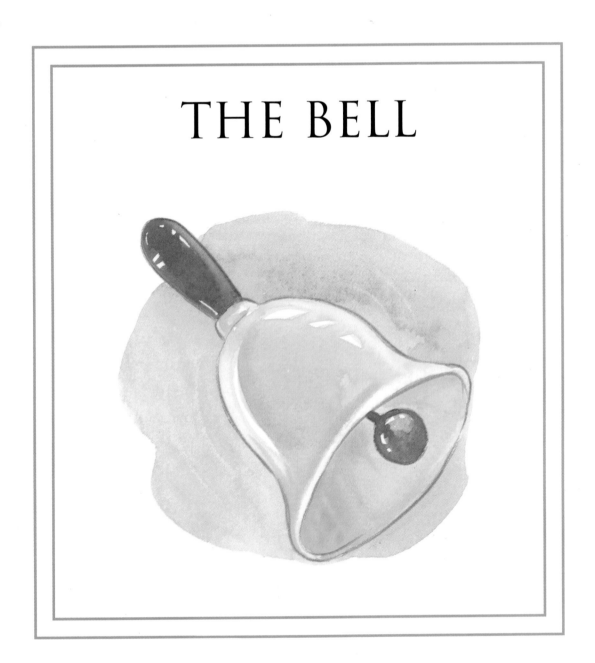

THE BELL

Teddy was bored. It had been raining all afternoon so he could not go out into the garden to play. Everyone else had found something to do but Teddy did not want to paint or read or do any of the things that the other toys were doing. He just sat on the toybox, staring at the rain through the window.

"There must be something I can do," he thought as he climbed down and went to see what he could find.

"There's not much here," he thought as he rummaged through the junk in the box under the table. Then he looked up and saw something on top of the table.

"Whatever is this?" he said, picking it up. Teddy had found a bell.

Ding! Dong! Clang! Clong! went the bell when he shook it. Teddy was delighted and walked round the room ringing the bell hard. The harder he shook it, the louder it rang.

"This is great fun!" he laughed as he rang the bell as loudly as he could. From all over the house the other toys came running up to Teddy.

"Oh dear! What's the matter? Where's the fire?" cried the toys. "Is somebody hurt? What's wrong?"

"There's nothing wrong," said Teddy, giggling. "I'm just ringing this old bell I found on the table." Teddy had thought it was very funny when the toys came running in.

"But you can't ring that bell if nothing's wrong and you don't need help," they said to Teddy. "That bell is not for playing with."

"We use that bell to call for help if one of us is in trouble," the rag doll said to Teddy. Then she took the bell from him and put it back on the table.

"Only ring it if you need some help," she said to Teddy.

The toys went back to what they were doing and left Teddy alone once more. He tried very hard not to think about the bell but he just could not resist it. He stood in front of the table and gazed at the bell.

"If I ring it very quietly they won't hear it," he thought as he lifted it down from the table. He just had to have another go.

Ding! Dong! rang the bell loudly. Ding! Dong!

The rag doll was the first to rush in to see who needed help but it was only Teddy playing with the bell again.

This time the rag doll said firmly to Teddy, "Leave that bell alone if you don't need help." Then she went out of the room. "It's all right," she said to the other toys. "It was just Teddy playing again. You can all go back to what you were doing because there's nothing wrong."

Teddy could not resist playing with the bell. He took it off the table and climbed right up to the top of the stairs with it.

"They won't hear me up here," he laughed to himself. Teddy stomped up and down at the top of the stairs ringing the bell as loudly as he could.

Teddy loved ringing the bell because it was so loud when he swung it round. Ding! Dong! Clang! Clang! Teddy danced around as he rang the bell, not looking where he was stepping and without realising he was dangerously near the edge of the stairs. He was laughing happily when he tripped and fell.

He tumbled and bounced down the stairs and got caught on a coat-hook that was sticking out of the wall.

"Oh, golly!" thought Teddy when he stopped moving. "How can I get down from here? I know, if I ring the bell someone will come and help me."

Teddy rang the bell as hard as he could but no-one came. The toys heard the bell but the rag doll said, "Take no notice. It's only Teddy playing."

Teddy was stuck on the hook. He rang the bell for a long time but still nobody came. Then, as he wriggled about trying to get free, he heard a funny tearing noise and felt something pulling at his fur. Teddy fell down from the hook still holding the bell. He looked at his side and saw some of his stuffing coming out where his fur had ripped on the hook! He felt very sorry for himself now.

"Oh what a silly bear I've been," he moaned. "If only I had not played with the bell someone would have come and helped me when I needed it."

He got up off the floor and, with one paw holding the bell and the other holding in his stuffing, he limped slowly back to the playroom.

Teddy put the bell back on the table and when the toys saw him again they were very surprised.

"What happened to you?" asked the rag doll, looking worried.

Teddy told her all about running off with the bell and falling down and getting stuck and ripping his fur.

"Here, let me see," she said and then went to get a needle and thread to mend him. The rag doll pushed Teddy's stuffing back in and sewed him up and soon he was as good as new.

"I'm sorry," said Teddy. "I promise I won't play with the bell again and will only use it if I need to."

"And next time we hear it we will all come and help," smiled the rag doll and all the other toys agreed.

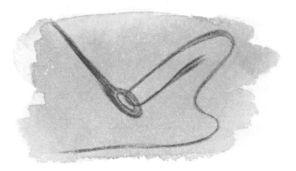

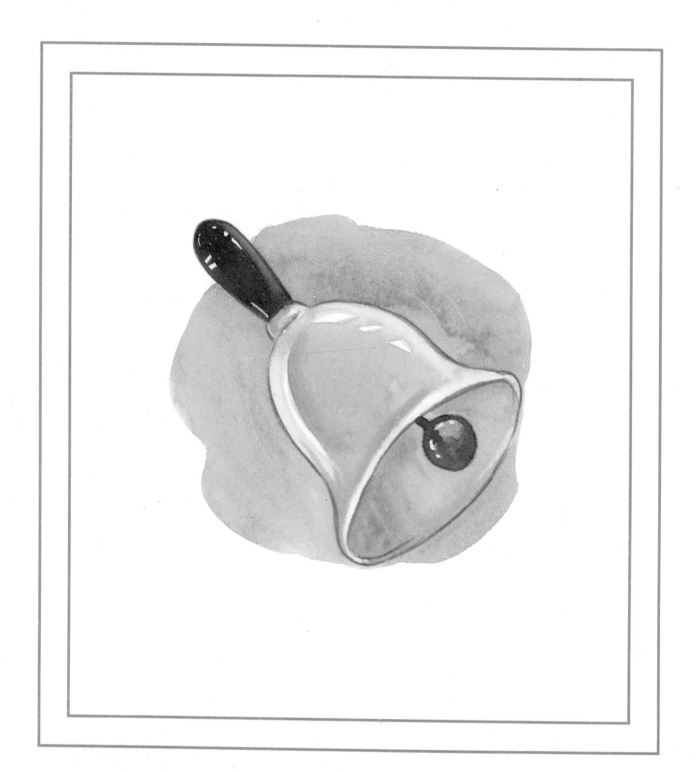

THE END